MARY HOFFMAN has written more than 70 books for children and in 1998 was made an Honorary Fellow of the Library Association for services to children and libraries. She is also the editor of a quarterly children's book review called *Armadillo*. Her book *Song of the Earth* (Orion) was shortlisted for the Kurt Maschler Award in 1995 and won the Primary English Award for that year. In 1992 *Amazing Grace*, her first book for Frances Lincoln, was selected for Child Education's Best Books of 1991 and Children's Books of the Year 1992, commended for the Kate Greenaway Medal, and included on the National Curriculum Reading List in 1996 and 1997. Its sequel, *Grace & Family*, was among Junior Education's Best Books of 1995 and was shortlisted for the Sheffield Libraries Book Award 1996. It was followed by *An Angel Just Like Me, A Twist in the Tail, Women of Camelot, Seven Wonders of the Ancient World, How to be a Cat* and a Grace story-book, *Starring Grace*. She has also collaborated with the illustrator Jackie Morris on *Parables: Stories Jesus Told, Miracles: Wonders Jesus Worked* and *Animals of the Bible*.

LYNNE RUSSELL was born in London, where she lives and works as an artist. Her work is inspired by the lifestyles and festivals of countries as far-flung as Mexico and India, and she has spent six months as artist-in-residence at the Cultural Museum in Chiapas, Southern Mexico. Her previous publications include *Neka goes to Market, Big Mama* and *Grandma Ghana* (both Heinemann International) and *One Smiling Grandma* (Reed). This is her first book for Frances Lincoln.

For Brendah Malahleka, who sent the Christmas card – M.H.
For my mother, and in loving memory of my father - L.R.

First published in Great Britain in 1999 by
Frances Lincoln Limited, 4 Torriano Mews
Torriano Avenue, London NW5 2RZ

www.franceslincoln.com

First paperback edition 2002

British Library Cataloguing in Publication Data
available on request

ISBN 0-7112-1423-9 hardback
ISBN 0-7112- 2022-0 paperback

Printed in Hong Kong
1 3 5 7 9 8 6 4 2

THREE WISE
WOMEN

Mary Hoffman
Illustrated by Lynne Russell

FRANCES LINCOLN

In the west, the sky was bright with stars as a young woman stayed up late, baking bread. As she waited for the dough to rise, she went to the door and combed her hair, singing a song about the moonlight.

Suddenly she stopped. Far away in the east there was a new star, brighter than all the rest. It was so bright that it bathed the woman's kitchen in star-shine. The beams from the star shone right on to the dough. The woman stared in disbelief – the dough was rising, as if filled with starlight.

She was afraid to touch it at first, but it was quite firm and ready to be baked. So she cooked it in the oven.

"As soon as it is ready," she said to herself, "I shall take the star-bread and travel east. I must find where the great light is coming from."

Way down in the south, where countries are hotter,
another woman sat up late at night rocking her child.
He was cutting a tooth and could not sleep. His mother
hummed to him and loved him with words that no one
else could understand.

"Shall Mama get you the moon, sweet baby?" she
crooned, taking her child out into the night to find
a breeze. "I could cut you a slice like a piece of mango
to cool your poor mouth."

The young child stretched out his fat little arms
to the moon and his mother laughed. Then they saw a
strange sight – a bright new star rising in the north-east.
Starlight shone on the child's face, making him smile.
His mother watched in silence. Her heart filled with
desire to leave her village and follow the bright star.

Far away in the south-east, an old woman was telling
stories to her grandchildren by the dying light of
a cooking fire.

Their mothers sat resting for the first time that day, while the old woman spoke of tigers and monkeys and temples and snakes and lotus flowers.

But gradually the story began to change and suddenly there was a star in it ... "Just like that star up there in the north-west," said the old woman.

"Then what happened, Grandma?" the children prompted her, for she had stopped in mid-story and was gazing at the star, till it filled her mind. And all the children hushed, and gazed with her, forgetting the story they had been listening to and wanting a new one, full of silver starlight.

What was it about that star? There was something
different about it, which drew all three women from
their homelands; and something the same, that said
to each of them, "Follow me."

They met on a path of starlight, not knowing how
long or far they had travelled. They were not hungry
or thirsty or tired, so each supposed her journey had
been short.

They found themselves on a dusty road at midnight,
where the sky was a deep dark blue and the moon
a fingernail of mother-of-pearl.

Each woman looked towards her own bright star,
which seemed to stand still over a huddle of houses.
   "The end of our journey," said the grandmother.
   "Let me carry your baby for a while," said the
young woman to the mother. And they all walked
together through the hills, past sleeping shepherds,
down to the town.

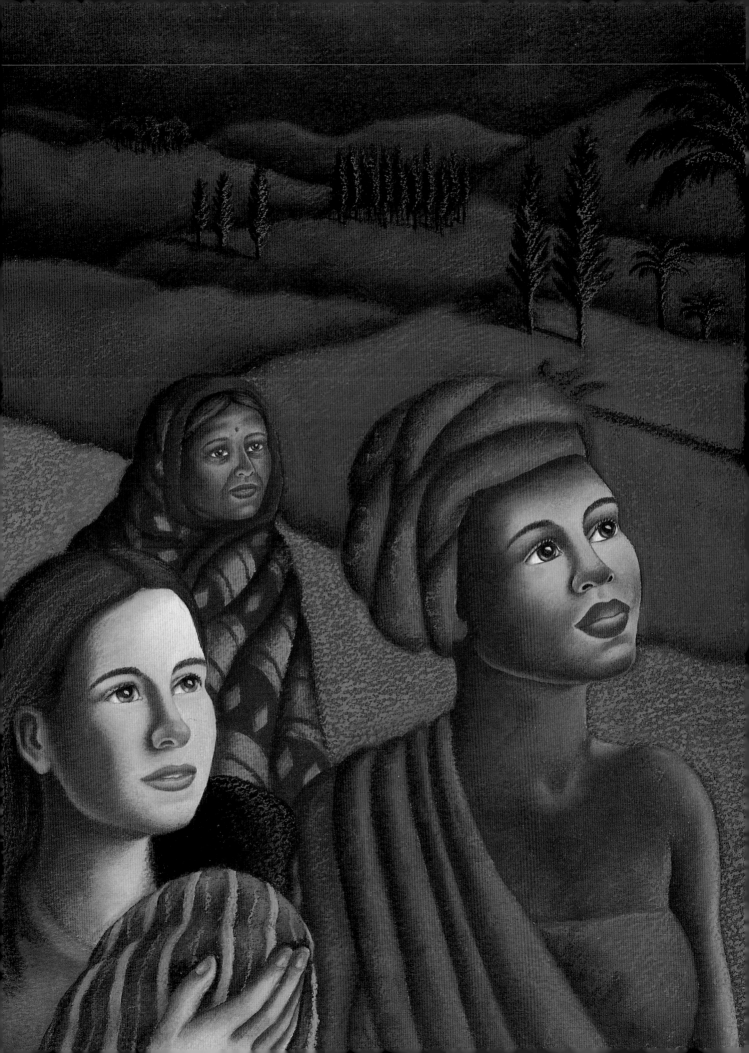

The star stayed where it was, growing ever bigger and brighter. It threw down great white spears of starlight on to a small white building with a thatched roof. The young woman started when she saw people coming out of the building and gave the baby back to his mother. They all watched as men in fine robes, and their servants, mounted on camels and rode away.

"Others have followed the star before us," said the mother. Suddenly all three women were afraid.

"We have come so far," said the young woman. "We must go inside."

They ducked their heads under the low door-beam and looked in. It was just a stable, with horses and donkeys. But it was also a home for a new family, a man and a woman and a newborn child all bathed in silver starlight. And there was gold too, a whole heap of it by the baby's makeshift crib, and other rich presents – but nothing was as rich or as bright as the glow surrounding the baby.

"Come in," said the new mother, and the women entered quietly. Their hearts were full. They too wanted to give presents.

They told the baby's mother how they had left their homes drawn by the star. They had travelled by star-path and moonlight, hardly knowing how they got there.

The young woman took the loaf of star-bread
from her bundle. It was still warm and smelled fresh.
She gave it to the baby's mother and, although he
was too young to eat it, the baby touched the loaf,
as if to bless it.

The grandmother said, "I have nothing in my bundle to give the child, but I would like to tell him a story."

Then the three women sat in the straw with the new family and the grandmother told a story full of starlight and hope.

And all the time, the mother from the south held her sleeping baby, and her heart was pounding, for he was all she had to give. And though she was filled with a strange new love for the baby in the crib, her own child was as dear to her as life itself.

When the story ended, her child awoke.
Straight away, he saw the baby and held
out his arms to him. The two mothers
held their sons and the child gave the
baby a kiss, full of starlight.

His mother sighed and held her child
tight. There had been a present after all.

The three wise women left the stable and walked the paths the star had made to lead them home. When they got back to their villages, no one noticed that they had been away. And no one remembered the star.

But the star-baby in the stable never forgot the women and their three presents. When he grew up, he showed that fresh-baked loaves taste even better when they are shared. He told the most wonderful stories to anyone who would listen. And the man whose birth had been marked by a new star taught the whole world that the greatest gift of all is love.

OTHER PICTURE BOOKS BY MARY HOFFMAN FROM FRANCES LINCOLN

AN ANGEL JUST LIKE ME
Illustrated by Cornelius Van Wright and Ying-Hwa Hu

When Tyler picks up a broken Christmas-tree angel, he asks,
"Why are they always pink? Aren't there any black angels?"
It's a question no one can answer – until Tyler
tells his friend Carl the problem.

ISBN 0-7112-1309-7

PARABLES: STORIES JESUS TOLD
Illustrated by Jackie Morris

In eight spirited retellings, Mary Hoffman shows how Jesus used simple
storytelling to explain God's idea of truth, fairness and love.
Jackie Morris's atmospheric illustrations bring alive the power
of the parables 2,000 years after they were first told.

ISBN 0-7112-1523-5

MIRACLES: WONDERS JESUS WORKED
Illustrated by Jackie Morris

Nine vibrant retellings show how Jesus overturned the laws of nature,
life and death, using his miraculous power to reflect God's great love
of humanity. Jackie Morris's illustrations help re-create
the wonders Jesus worked.

ISBN 0-7112-1814-5

Frances Lincoln titles are available from all good bookshops.
You can also buy books and find out more about your favourite titles,
authors and illustrators at our website: www.franceslincoln.com.